The Chronicles of Corillium

Imperial Peril

2017

Authors

Daniel J. Breen and Tristram Ross

Book I

The Chronicles of Corillium: Imperial Peril

First published 2017

Published by Kallis Publishing

Email: kallispublishing@gmail.com

Original illustrations by Dennis

Printed by Lulu

First Edition

The Chronicles of Corillium: Imperil Peril

Breen, Daniel J. and Ross, Tristram

ISBN: 978-0-6481960-0-6

Dedication:

To all those that have been lost to war, whether it be on a battlefield or of the mind. We all have our personal struggle, of which many do not return unscathed. It is due to this that this book is dedicated to all those we have lost to the struggle of life.

Chapter 1

A Glimmer of Hope

Inhale... exhale... inhale... exhale...

Dawn's chest rises and falls softly, her eyes closed tightly, her face covered in a fine dust as she slowly begins to awake. Her head pounding to its own tribal beat from the impact of her fall. Dust and ash falling like snow all around her as she slowly looks up to the ceiling. *No!* The floor she was standing on only moments ago. Where was she now? Where were the documents? The ones she had searched for so long to find the final key to her project. The empire's records of births and deaths.

"Shit," Dawn groans as she punches the ground in frustration before wailing in anguish. Her entire life, all of it leads to nothing. She will die for nothing at the bottom of this pit, in a ruined basement of a crumbling building, in an infested city. The capital of a war torn country and empire. Slowly rising to her feet and shielding her eyes, a wave of heat washed over her. Looking up to see the flames eating up the roof of the building, a flash of recognition crosses her mind. She had found the records. They were in her hands. Dawn looks down at her hands and winces, noticing her dislocated ring finger. Reaching for it, she closes her eyes and forces it back into place causing her to cry out in pain. Checking her armour, she finds a wooden stake stuck into her side. Luckily, it had only just penetrated the armour and left a small gash. Sighing softly, she tears the stake out of her armour, flinching slightly before looking around the rubble and mess. "What happened? I was so close. I just had them." she yells to no one. Her only response is the creaking of strained supports holding up what remained of the roof, and the burning inferno consuming the floor above. Dawn began to dig through the rubble in a frantic search. "Where is it?" she growls vehemently before a loud creaking sound echoes around the basement.

Dawn's head snaps up just in time to see another support beam give way, bringing with it roof tiles and stone tumbling down towards her. Diving to the side she screams in pain as a large wooden beam strikes her across the back pinning her to the floor. Whimpering softly, she looks to the jeweled bracelet on her arm, gifted to her by Riven, her beloved friend and Cousin.

Beginning to sob softly, "I am sorry, I should have waited. I should have listened. I am sorry. But I needed it, I had to find who I am, where I came from."

Rubbing her eyes pathetically, she slowly begins to try and pull her way out from underneath the beam. Every fibre of her being screaming at her to stay put, and just give in. "No! People depend on me, children, families, and my family!" she shouts at the top of her lungs. Her shout becoming a loud growl as she heaves herself up and pushes the beam off, before collapsing back to her knees in exhaustion.

She was free, and she could escape. Thrusting her hand out in front of her, she tries to focus on her Celestial magic's and tear a rift in essence of reality to connect two separate spots on Kallis through a portal. A bead of bloody sweat forms above her brow before she gasps in pain as her concentration is overwhelmed by the throbbing pain of her head. Growling in frustration, she looks up at the sky through the ruined roof and calls out at the top of her lungs, "It's no use. all of this... a waste!"

Looking back down and kicking one of the fallen support beams with as much force as she can muster, grimacing in the pain of the impact, her eyes glance over something. Frowning for a brief moment, realisation washes over her, the roof collapsing had made a ramp, a ramp she could climb. Summoning the rest of her strength, Dawn pushes herself up off the ground and scrambles her way up to the next floor. Only two feet in front of her lay her staff, her arcane focus the tool to which she channels her more powerful spells. Lunging forward, she grabs it pausing, an expression of horror crossing her face as she looks around. The entire rooms' engulfed in flames, no exit, no escape. Swallowing softly, rivulets of blood trickle down her face. She pulls herself up out of the hole and stands upright, resting some of her weight on her staff as her eyes scan the room looking for any way out.

Closing her eyes for a few long moments. *Inhale, exhale, inhale and exhale,* her eyes snap open, focusing on a single spot in the room, glaring at it with determination, a new fire igniting; not one of flames, but of the burning desire to live, to succeed, a glimmer of hope.

Chapter 2

Flames of Oblivion

In the corner of the room, was a pillar, supporting most of the remaining ceiling. Smirking slightly, Dawn takes a few steps back and laughs uncontrollably. "Not here to get me out of trouble this time Cousin. Guess I will have to get myself into more." She jokes to the crackling inferno around her.

Holding her staff tightly, her knuckles turn white as she directs her staff towards the pillar. Closing her eyes, she begins to channel her magic muttering a few words of prayer to her gods. Her eyes snap open. Her body coursing with energy, spinning her staff around and taking two quick steps forward, she hurls the energy out of her staff sending a spinning ball of Magical energy towards the pillar. A loud crack echoing around the nearby streets as the base of the pillar explodes sending shards of white stone everywhere. Shielding her eyes, Dawn tenses in preparation of what is to come as the roof collapses around her, praying to all that she knows.

Blinking slowly, Dawn opens her eyes and looks around at the mountain of smouldering rubble around her. Beginning to laugh, she looks up at the dark skies in disbelief. "I am alive. That actually worked. That actually worked," shaking her head, blinking a few times remembering the floor she is standing on has already collapsed beneath her once already she jumps up onto the rubble and climbs her way to freedom, grimacing every so often, as unextinguished flames sear at her skin, and heat up her armour. Climbing to the crest of what was once the wall of the building, Dawn collapses over the side tumbling down and crashing into an abandoned cart in the middle of the road. "Alive! Free! That's something I suppose." She murmurs quietly before looking around a little, her vision blurring as she reaches up and dabs her hand to her hairline. Looking at her bloodied gauntlets, she frowns slightly. "Oh! I must have hit my head harder than I thought." she murmurs in a slur before her head lolls to one side, blackness closing in, encompassing her entirely.

Dawn stands in the centre of a wide open expanse of nothingness. The oblivion of unconsciousness slowly subsiding. Blinking in confusion, she looks down and frantically pats herself down. "All in one piece, but where am I? And why am I talking to myself?" Dawn grimaces painfully as if by reminder her head starts gushing blood, as a thumping headache pounds the inside of her skull. Thump! Thump! Thump! Each thump becoming louder and louder. A splitting headache from a concussion. The sound suddenly stopped. Then the floor was gone. Dawn screamed at the top of her lungs but there was no air to breathe. Where had it gone? It had been consumed. Consumed by fire. All of a sudden, Dawn lands in a heap on the bottom of a black pit. She looks around frantically. Slowly little glimpses of light begun to ignite, one after the other. All of them flames. They had taken the air, consumed it, to create more life. More flames of oblivion. Is that where she was? The plane of the damned? If only she could just think straight. What can she do? How can she escape? She had been here only moments ago on a floor, then in a pit burning. She had escaped, she was free. Or was she dead? No, she should be in the sacred hunting ground. She wasn't dead! Captured? Imprisoned? Just think Dawn, think! Where are you?

"Wake up." murmurs a frightened little voice.

Dawn turns around suddenly, "Who said that? Where are you? Show yourself!" she screams a hint of panic in her voice as the flames continue to grow near her.

"Wake up" the timid voice repeats.

Dawn's entire world shifts violently from side to side. What now? An earthquake? Wait, no! That voice. Riven? No, too young. A child, one of the orphans? No, it couldn't be, not here in Damnation. No, not Damnation. Kallis? Celestial city? Yes! She was in The Empire of Man. The Celestial city, laying in the street.

"Wake up! They are coming..." Her voice falters in fear.

Chapter 3

The Girl

Dawn's eyes snap wide open with realisation. It had been a dream. A figment of her imagination, a hallucination, that her brain had conjured up while she had been unconscious. The voice kept nagging at the oblivion. The voice was in trouble. Someone needed her help.

Dawn throws herself forward and gasps for breath. Her arms flailing about sending a little girl sprawling backward onto the cobblestones. "Don't hurt me" the little girl begs as she begins to scramble along the ground to get away from Dawn.

Shaking her head frantically to try and throw the remnants of drowsiness off. Dawn manages a few words of comfort. "I won't..." she murmurs in a weakened voice, blinking twice to clear her head as she looks to her right just in time to spot the shadows dancing across the wall nearing the corner. Scooping the child up into her arms and grabbing her staff, she sprints. Not looking behind her she just runs and runs, "We are going to be alright. We just need to run" she murmurs to the girl in her arms as she skids around bend after bend.

Skidding to a stop, Dawn bends over slightly and pants heavily, blood blurring her vision as it slowly cascades its way down her face. Wiping it out of the way she looks at the girl in her arms and manages a small and exhausted smile of reassurance, "We... will be alright... we... just need to hide... and rest." she manages to say breathlessly. Looking behind her, Dawn saw an overpass bridge connecting two buildings either side of the streets. Mind racing, she looks around then back down the way she had come, a hulking shadow slowly edging its way around the final bend towards them. The little girl shrinks into Dawn closing her eyes tightly and beginning to tremble in fear "It... it's coming." she mumbles with chattering teeth.

Swallowing softly, Dawn watches as the looming giant slowly makes its way into view, the mass of decaying flesh held together with dark and forbidden magic, a thousand flies surrounding it, drawn by the foul stench of death and horror that followed the fleshy construct known as an abomination. It's horrendous face falling apart as its ghostly eyes lock onto the small human in the middle of the street. Stretching its arms, it roars, a bone chilling cry of anger, its right hand bursting into flames as the metal enchanted maul springs to life, beginning to pick up its pace, the monster bounds down the street towards its prey. The earth trembles with every step of its humongous form.

Dawn blinks, a second passing, her vision snapping from the flesh abomination bounding towards her to the quaking ground, she blinks again, another second gone, her head snapping to her route of escape calculating her chances of outrunning the beast. Blink, her heart rate slows her legs, stiffen the blood draining from her face in fear. Blink.

Dawn looks to the trembling form of the girl in her arms. What was the girl's name? Where was her family? This poor child, doomed to live in this damned city. To save a stranger passed out on the street. Only to die in that same city on a different street, clinging to that stranger as they're run down by a beast that should only belong to nightmares. Blink. her eyes snap back to the abomination, soon it would be upon them. Soon they would be in the embrace of their gods. Well, at least this girl would be, she would make it to a better place. One, where she was loved. Where she would be cared for by the Fa'en. Too young. She would die. She could only be four maybe five years old, her beautiful features, her long brown hair, her lovely eyes saddened by fear. *If only I could see her smile, she would have a smile of an angel I am sure.*

Dawn's hand tightens around her staff once more as she blinks a final time. Five seconds had passed. Five seconds she had stood still, her mind racing, her heart slowing, her vision clearing. For five seconds, Dawn had let her body prepare itself for what is to come. For what is next. Thrusting her staff into the air, Dawn shouted at the top of her lungs, "You saved me. Now, let me save you!" she roars in defiance. The world slows for a single moment, a well of power swells in the storming sky before a horrendous clap echoes across the city as an object begins falling from the Cosmos. Bringing her staff down, Dawn points it directly at the overpass. Her eyes glowing blue, her form pulsating with magic as she mutters incoherently in the tongue of the Prima; the mythically legendary first people of Kallis. Those that first shaped the words of power into mortal tongues.

A large shooting star hurtles down faster and faster leaving a trail of smoke and smouldering rocks behind it. It impacts with an ear shattering crash. Dawn quickly turns away from the impact and the beast shielding the girl and her ears, as a wave of air, dust and rocks washes over them sending Dawn sprawling to the ground. Huddling protectively around the child she whispers, "It's going to be alright. We will make it. I won't let them get you."

Dawn mutters over and over into the girl's ear before the dust finally settles. Slowly relaxing her form, she lays flat rolling over to look up at the sky, then to the girl whilst turning her away from the sight of the impact. Her innocent eyes had seen far too much already. No need for her to see more than she needs to.

Glancing over her shoulder once, to make sure the monster was no longer a threat, Dawn gives a little nod and finally lets out a small sigh of relief, picking the girl back up and beginning to limp her way forward through the city "One less monstrosity of the Daegon in Kallis... only an infinite number of them to go." Muttering under her breath, she offers her first genuine friendly smile to the girl, "Hi! My name is Dawn. What's yours?"

The girl looks at Dawn for a few moments as if deciding whether or not she can be trusted, then looking over Dawn's shoulder too late to see the destruction left behind them. The girl peers back at the woman carrying her, swallowing nervously, she mumbles in a shy and fearful tone, "I. my... m-my name is Ameliana."

Chapter 4

Haven

Smiling warmly, Dawn gives a little nod. "Nice to meet you Ameliana, we make quite the team don't we? Now, what do you say we find somewhere safe to rest a while? Would you like that?" Dawn manages in the most cheerful and warm tone her hurting and exhausted body is capable of. Ameliana responds with a little and rapid nod of her head before hugging Dawn. Clinging onto the armoured mage for dear life.

Dawn smiles softly and gives her a little comforting pat before looking to a relatively untouched house. Walking over to it, she places her shoulder against the door and heaves her weight against it, pushing it open. Staff first, she slowly walks in her eyes darting around the dark interior for any sign of threat. Finding none, she walks to the far wall and sits Ameliana down. "I will be right back, I am just going to close the door and make sure we weren't seen." Waiting for a moment to see if Ameliana understood. Moving to the door and peeking outside quickly, Dawn then pushes the door closed as quietly as possible. Leaning her head against the wooden door, she mutters something about how nice a comfortable bed would be before she limps her way back over to Ameliana. Resting her back against the wall, she just lets herself fall sliding down the wall before she lands with a soft thud on the wooden floorboards. "Well, let's try and get some rest. Alright?" She says in a seemingly cheerful tone before she wraps one arm around Ameliana. Holding her staff close, she closes her eyes slowly before letting her head loll forward as sleep and exhaustion soon overcome her.

***

A woman clad in black leather, waltzes over to Dawn watching her curiously as she snoozes under the white leafed tree. A teasing smirk soon crosses the woman's lips before she kneels down and pinches Dawn's nose and begins counting.

Dawn lunges forward gasping for breath, her eyes snapping awake looking up at the woman she growls softly, "Riven..." she whines before blinking a few times and looking up and squinting at the light. "I was sleeping." she complains, before eyeing Riven accusingly.

Riven stands upright again and giggles softly, "You should have seen your face, and besides, it's 2 hours past midday. No time for sleeping. Look around, it's a perfect day!" she proclaims before looking at Dawn expectantly.

Dawn rolls her eyes and stretches her limbs before sitting her hands in her lap and looking at Riven rather unamused, "Remind me to wake you up first thing in the morning," she says mockingly.

Shrugging slightly Riven gestures at her gear, "I was in the Legion. I doubt you could possibly wake me up earlier than I used to during my training, and besides you couldn't get yourself up that early if your life depended on it." she teases before offering her hand down towards Dawn.

Dawn rolls her eyes, "I could too." she retorts before reluctantly taking Riven's hand and pulling herself up off the ground, brushing her robe off. "So, you said today was perfect. What's so perfect about it?" Dawn says challengingly a teasing smirk upon her lips.

Riven smiles knowingly and simply leans forward whispering something in Dawn's ear then takes a step back, a look upon her face as if to say 'and?'

Dawn reddens in the cheek profusely before she leans forward and responds in kind then grins broadly at Riven.

Shaking her head Riven begins laughing, "Hey now, it's not a competition, and besides if it was, I would win." she teases before winking playfully at Dawn. She wraps one arm around her and begins guiding Dawn down towards the riverside. "It's a beautiful afternoon that shouldn't be wasted sleeping it away. So we are going to go for a swim!" Riven says quite decisively giving Dawn, no room for argument.

Dawn eyes Riven for a few moments before smirking at her, "Oh you think you would win. Mmh perhaps you would win, but only because I let you." Dawn retorts before giving a happy nod of her head glancing up at the canopy of the forest, as they make their way from the Lyeis estate down to the banks of the Caliane River.

"I love... this place. It really is home isn't it." Dawn lets out a little happy sigh, slipping out of her boots as they reach the small sandy beach. Leaving them on the grass before she begins to walk forward tossing her clothing to the side, then runs out into the water and dives in.

Riven watches Dawn head into the water and laughs softly before disrobing out of her black leather armour and rushing to catch up. Diving into the water just as Dawn surfaces splashing her cousin in a watery spray before surfacing herself. Wiping the water out of her eyes, her damp white hair slick against the sides of her face, she beams at Dawn. "Water a bit cold, is it?" Riven teases giving Dawn a little nod.

Dawn looks down then frowns, "Hey! It's almost winter okay." She retorts before narrowing her eyes at Riven, grinning deviously, "And I will show you cold." she promises before launching herself at Riven tackling her into the cool water.

***

Dawn laid upon her back. The sand keeping her back warm as she rolls onto her side looking at Riven, "That was an amazing swim."

Staying on her back Riven opens one eye and glances over to Dawn and smirks, "And you wanted to sleep the afternoon away." she teases before rolling onto her side returning Dawn's gaze.

"Well, in my defence I was having quite a dream." offers a little shrug, "Although it didn't compete with this afternoon. So, thank you. Also, I think we both learnt that I am the better swimmer of the two of us."

Riven raises her eyebrow slightly and props her head up resting it on her arm, "Oh! Is that so? If I recall, you were the one that almost drowned."

Dawn scoffs, "Oh! Don't lie. You were impressed with how deep I managed to go and how long I can hold my breath." she retorts eyeing Riven knowingly.

Riven gives a little nod, "True, but still, I would rather not let you drown." she points out before adding, "And it was quite impressive. I really must ask where you learnt such magical skills." she teases.

Dawn giggles softly before rolling back onto her back, "I have had a lot of practice. Some half Imperial, half Arcadian cousin of mine. Can't quite remember her name. I think it might start with an R. Yeah that sounds about right. Rachel Arashiha?" giving a mocking nod of her head before grinning teasingly at Riven.

Riven looks mock offended, "What! You mean there is another cousin and you didn't tell me? All this time, I thought I was your only cousin." She pouts sadly and turns onto her side then adds sideways, "Well, you know, the only cousin besides my brother but he doesn't count." she teases.

Dawn tsks playfully at Riven, "Oh don't be like that my dear, dear cousin. I still have room in my life for you. It will just be different now." Dawn teases before reaching across and giving Riven's bare back a little shove. "Now, it's getting late. I will race you back to the estate." Dawn challenges before she scrambles to her feet and sprinted off into the forest. "Oh and last one home has to cook dinner!" she calls out.

Riven scrambles to her feet as well, looking around the beach at their discarded drying clothing. She looks up at Dawn as she runs off. "What about our clothes?" she calls out before completely forgetting about the clothes, at hearing the threat of having to cook the dinner herself. "Hey, No fair! wait for me!" Riven calls out before sprinting after Dawn.

***

Dawn looks down at the ball of oatmeal in front of her, the colour draining from her face as she looks up at Riven. "You don't call this food, right?"

Riven smirks at her, "Well, you never said what food I had to cook, and besides it was good enough for me when I was in the Legion. So it's good enough for when I am not." Riven beams cheerfully before beginning to happily eat away at her own bowl of oatmeal.

Grumbling softly, Dawn moves the pile of sludge that is pretending to be food around in her bowl before looking at Riven accusingly, "Didn't I teach you how to cook?" she scolds.

Riven gives a little nod, "You did."

"Then what is this!" she proclaims in defiance.

"That is why you should learn to wait for me. I did say so."

Dawn looks at Riven blankly for a few moments, "I hate you." she simply responds.

Riven raises her eyebrow and begins laughing, "No, you don't, you love me." she teases in response.

Dawn inclines her head to one side, "True. I will get you back for this you know."

Riven laughs softly again, "mhm. I'm sure you will." she retorts in a seemingly uncaring fashion as she continues to happily eat away at her food before returning to Dawn. "Not hungry?" she teases.

"Ah... I think I might just go to bed." Dawn says cautiously pushing her bowl towards the centre of the table.

Riven grins teasingly, "But didn't you spend half the day sleeping? Then you demand that I make you dinner and you don't even try it." Riven pouts playfully at Dawn before giggling softly, "Have a good night Dawn. I won't be far behind", she says cheerfully feeling quite happy at having won this round.

Dawn eyes Riven accusingly before dragging her feet towards the door to her room, "You know, remind me to wait for you next time."

Riven snickers softly, "I thought I just did." she teases.

Rolling her eyes, Dawn walks over to her bed and flops down onto the soft mattresses letting sleep once again encompass her in its embrace.

Chapter 5

Awakening

Dawn stirs in her sleep, a small cloud of dust falling from the ceiling of the ruined building, her arm involuntarily pulls Ameliana closer, holding her protectively, her ears twitching slightly, her senses picking up on danger even before she awakes. Beginning to slide to one side, her armoured chest plate scraping loudly along the stone wall before she falls to one side with a small thump.

The creaking sound of floorboards is heard from around the corner as three Legionnaires, Loyal to the Regency that caused the Daegon invasion appeared, standing over the sleeping woman and child. Drawing their swords, they approach the pair, a wicked grin across the first, and bloodlust in his eyes as he draws his sword back in preparation before his eyes go wide in pain. Dawn had grabbed her staff and thrust it up at his chest, muttering something under her breath before a shockwave of power shoots out of her staff, hitting the Legionnaire at point blank and blowing him across the room through the stone masonry wall out onto the street. Blinking slowly, Dawn's blood begins to pump, her heart racing, vision focusing. Time slowing, her mind calculating every possibility, one down two left, two swords one is going to hit either the child or her, not even a question of who. Grinning stupidly, Dawn grabs Ameliana by the arm and all but yanks her over her own body and tosses her to the side, narrowly avoiding the first sword as it thuds harmlessly into the now vacant floor space. Springing into action before clank. Dawn's eyes widen in fear as she looks down at the sword buried into her stomach,

"I, b-but she is so young. Don't hurt her, please." The armoured legionnaire tries to rip his sword out of Dawn only managing to pull the impaled woman forward sprawling her across the ground, bleeding profusely as she had to act quickly.

Her heart racing, slowing her vision, blurring her, life draining from her body, grunting in effort, she pulls herself to sit upright bracing against the wall. She just laughs softly, "You told me to wait, when will I learn to listen?" she murmurs before tears begin to roll down her face. "I failed. I died. I am sorry my love. I failed you and her." Glancing over to the terrified form of Ameliana cowering in the darkened corner, she was thrown into, murmuring the words breathlessly, "I am sorry." Dawn mutters before her head slumps forward and she exhales, her chest heaving as her last breath leaves her body.

Two Arrows fly through the man sized hole made in the house, felling one Legionnaire instantly and piercing through the other's ankle and all but nailing him to the floor. Walking through the door her hips swaying in an over exaggerated manner, her figure clads in tight fitting dark leather armour, a cruel smirk on her face as she walks up to the Legionnaire and tsks at him, "Now, you are a silly one. Aren't you?" she taunts as she draws out one of her long ceremonial daggers and drags the flat of it over his chest plate, "Going and killing my target. What am I going to do with you now? Perhaps I should throw you to Empress Regent, or the Coven, or perhaps even my brother?" Tilting her head to one side, her eyes were remorseless as she places the dagger against his throat, "Or shall I be merciful and take your life here and now?"

The Legionnaire trembles in terror at the sight of the woman in front of him, the signature appearance, the stories, though she was gone, a myth, surely not real, she had disappeared, she had died, this couldn't be her. The thoughts racing through the Legionnaire's mind stumbling over each other to find the truth.

Grinning devilishly at the legionnaire, she tsks toyingly at him, "Now, now, don't tell me you don't know who I am?" pouting playfully, "Surely you know?" batting her eyelashes at him, "Come now. Cat got your tongue?" rolling her eyes before drawing the blade across the Legionnaire's neck slicing his throat open from ear to ear. Looking back out of the building to the other women gathered outside, she points at the dead woman on the floor, "Take her, and make sure she is alive when I return."

The other women bow their heads before seeming to wash over the street and into the house gathering around Dawn's lifeless body and hauling her up into the air. Supported by them all and like a collection of wraiths, they slink out into the street and deeper into the city.

The woman watches the others leave before looking over at the child hiding in the corner. Walking over her footfalls echoing on the wooden floor as she kneels down in front of the child and smiles slightly at her, "Hello... What's your name... hmm...?"

The girl trembles in fear at the woman looking over to the dead Legionnaires on the floor, "I... I am Ameliana... who... Who are you?... Are you going to hurt me? Where are you taking her?"

Glancing back over her shoulder to ensure no one else is present. The woman stands back up and returns her dagger to her belt and smiles softly, "No. I won't hurt you and she is being taken away. As to whom I am, that's easy." Smirking slightly, "I am the Black Witch." she says simply.

Chapter 6

The Black Witch

Ameliana looked up the Black Witch with wide round eyes, "C-can I go with her? Will she be alright? Sh-she s-saved me." Tears filled her soulful eyes, full of worry and terror. Instinctively, the woman reached out and crushed the child to her breast, holding her comfortingly and stroking her hair.

"You poor child, Ameliana, you have seen too much in your few years, but you are strong, so strong." Pulling her away to look the girl in the eyes she began, "So is she. Dawn Arashiha is one of the strongest women I know, and she will be alright. But those men hurt her, badly. I have a few things to say about that." She states, her silver eyes flashing menacingly. "For now, you will come with me. They would keep you, train you. If that is to be your destiny, it will be your choice. I know of others assaulting the city would see you to safety, stay close to me little one, and if I tell you to close your eyes. Do so." The Witch rose to her feet, the tight fitting black leather creaking slightly, she pulled her gauntlets tighter and swept her snowy hair back away from her grim face. Collecting her bow, she reached down and took the girl's hand, giving it a comforting squeeze. "I have been looking for your saviour for some time. Very clever of her to show me the way by throwing that bad man through the wall, hmm…? Her redecorating also makes a nice door out to the streets. Stay low, stay quiet."

The Black Witch lead the way rolling her feet expertly to mask the sound of her passing. Crouching low to diminish her silhouette. Ameliana did her best to mimic the movement, stepping where her guide stepped, trying not to disturb the rubble and attract attention. The Celestial city was in flames, thick choking smoke hung in the air limiting visibility. In the distance, a monstrous inhuman roar reverberated off of the buildings, its echoes chilling the blood, and causing Ameliana to tremble in fear. At the sound the Witch changed their path immediately, heading in the opposite direction and right into a party of five Loyalist Legion soldiers, searching for their fallen comrades. The cruel warriors drew their Naernian steel swords immediately and advanced, but the Black Witch was unperturbed, her anger at what she had just witnessed fuelling a desire for this confrontation. Pushing Ameliana behind her, she adopted a wide stance and thrust her hands out before her and overhead. "Fear Me!" she commanded, and the smoke before her swirled around several black shapes that burst forth suggesting to the mind of an observer, bones and claws, fangs and imminent horrific death. With a terrifying screech, heard perhaps externally, perhaps only in the mind, the darkness sped to meet the Legionnaires head on with the flapping of bat-like wings. The Legionnaires did not flinch at first, raising shields and slashing forth bravely, but the shrieks became mocking, and the claws began to rip and tear. As one, all five turned and fled, retreating in panic, their coordination lacking and leaving them exposed, easy prey to a skilled archer who knew the weak points in their armour. The Witches bow twanged rhythmically, the arrows following a pale purple glowing trail to the gaps in the Legionaries' armour felling them in short order. The shadowy creatures swarmed the corpses in a flurry of movement, ultimately burrowing inside and disappearing from sight. The corpses were no more than shrivelled desiccated husks, twisted in poses of agony. "I'm sorry, I should have told you to hide your eyes. They shouldn't have stabbed her" she growled cruelly. Ameliana stared transfixed at the corpses and merely nodded her agreement, seeming satisfied as to the fate of the men.

After several blocks, avoiding further pursuit, they took shelter a moment in the hollow of the burnt husk of what was once a fine clothier's shop. Feeling momentarily secure, Ameliana's sweet innocent voice pierced the oppressive silence, "Who were those women who took Dawn?" she asked quietly, "Were they witches like you?"

Regarding the child with the penetrating stare of her silver eyes, she reached out to wipe clean a smudge of ash on the child's face, nodding slowly. "They are witches, but not quite like me. They are sisters, members of the coven that trained me. Their specialties are more toward seeking, and healing, where I am more dangerous. But not to you little one, fear not."

Ameliana looked at her defiantly, "I am not afraid of you. But they should be." She spoke vehemently inclining her head in the direction of the dead Legionnaires.

Chuckling darkly, her lips peeling into a wide grin, the Black Witch responded, "Yes. Yes, they should. I like you Ameliana. You are a good judge of character and have a cool head. Let's get you to safety, shall we?" She offered, pushing off of the wall where her dark leathers blended so well with the charred wood, flowing out into the street, the child hurrying to follow. Their path, however, was not without obstacles. Nearing the corner at the end of the street, the Witch and the child tried to hug the building to remain unseen but the raging fires had weakened the structure causing it to collapse. Grabbing the little girl, the pair fled to the middle of the square away from the cascading rubble, leaving them totally exposed and in full view of nearly 10 full squads of the Loyalist Legion and their pet. Beyond could be seen several other squads and the glow of fire abominations. Ameliana froze in terror, gazing up at the monstrosity that had been terrorising them with its hungry roaring. An enormous Rakath, a lizard like Daegon, as tall as the largest buildings in the city, its scaly tail sweeping aside the stone and timber of fallen buildings, as it twitched back and forth in eager anticipation. The beasts elongated maw opened wide, revealing row upon row of dagger like teeth as it roared a challenge. In unison, more than 50 Loyalist Legion soldiers, drew steel and their commanders pointed blades at the pair. Ameliana clung to the witch's leg whimpering and sealing her eyes shut awaiting their doom.

A fell wind blew through the city, swirling in circles about the Black Witch and her companion as she weaved her hands in ritualistic patterns. Her white hair whipped about her as her eyes locked on the glowing red eyes of the enormous Rakath. Her voice rang clearly and with confidence, sounding more like multiple voices speaking in unison, echoing each other, "Aezeranum Calachthi Surunaman Kethketchi! Aezeri Morgothuul! I know what you are and know your name! I invoke the pacts of old and bind your will to my own. Serve me Aezeri Morgothuul, I command it!" she cried at the top of her lungs. The Rakath roared in rage and defiant anger, pitting its will against the tiny black clad woman. The contest was short, fuelled by the need for survival and to protect the child, there was only one chance and no backing down. The great beast bowed its head in reluctant acquiescence. A wicked smile curling her lips, "Feed! Feed on these men, your former masters, devour them and those of their ilk, then return home and trouble Kallis no more!" she commanded. At her words, the Legionnaire's paused, the less disciplined among them casting a glance over their shoulders, the last moves they would ever make. The Rakath tore into the Legionnaires with abandon ripping and tearing at those it once served, their screams of agony echoing through the ruined streets of the Imperial City.

The Black Witch wasted no time, scooping up the little girl, she turned and ran sprinting with all her strength back the way they had come. "They never learn," She murmured smugly. But their flight was short lived. Archers among the legions loosed their arrows at her in the hope that their deaths would be avenged, and arrows rained over the fleeing pair. Searing pain flooded the white haired witch's senses as a trio of arrows penetrated her, one in the shoulder, another her side, and the last through her calf, sending Witch and child alike tumbling to the ground. Undeterred the witch crawled, forcing down the pain and nausea brought on by shock, toward a fissure in the ground through which poured forth a familiar cloud of darkness. Dragging the girl with her, the Witch lowered her into the fissure and tumbled in behind, the dark cloud gripping the stone above and sealing it shut. They fell impossibly slowly, cushioned by the darkness landing at the feet of an ancient seeming woman, her stick like limbs extending to admonish the Witch and her charge with a crooked finger. In a rasping croak, the aged woman spoke, "You bring trouble and strangers to our door. You command those you have no right to lead anymore. You tax our resources and expose us to those who destroy. Bold child. You were always bold, but can you justify your rashness this time? I always look forward to the sass in your guilty explanations. Welcome home, Riven."

Panting for breath and wincing in pain as she bled from her wounds, "Thank you mother, you are looking well, have you lost weight?" She smirked. "Where is the one I sent ahead?"

The old woman frowned down at the bloody Black Witch, "Sass, sass indeed. She is with the bone menders, and the wraith watchers were sent to find you. Lucky for you, I allowed it. So full of holes. What did I tell you about getting yourself full of holes? Foolish girl. The one we have, she is the one you told us about? And who is the child? You bring us a new recruit?" The old woman's frail appearance was belied by her commanding tone and authoritative presence.

Riven nodded, "Dawn. Is she alright? Tell me she has been revived! And this, this is Ameliana. She is not a mere foundling; she is our daughter. Her training here is not mine to offer." She lied smoothly.

The old woman narrows her eyes in annoyance and suspicion, "Hmmm. Very well. But I think I know the price, your friend, your cousin, will pay for her healing." She rasped her mouth curling into a wicked grin. Riven merely smirked and nodded up at her mentor, the head of the coven, her spiritual mother, so much the opposite of her natural one, before she passed out from loss of blood.

Chapter 7

The Inner Sanctum

Ameliana found herself in the middle of a heptagonal chamber, carved from the dark natural deposit of marble, at the heart of the mountain the Coven of Imperial, witches called home. Her tiny hand was locked in the vice-like yet comforting grip, of the claw-like nearly skeletal hand, of the ancient frail seeming woman that everyone in the series of caverns referred to as Mother. The cloying scent of herbs, dried flowers, and the decaying body parts of creatures mundane and exotic, bound together, in complex fetishes, hanging at strategic locations around the room, overwhelmed her senses causing her to wrinkle her nose. To either side of her was a raised platform of colourless crystals upon which lay the unconscious form of the women, who could be twins save for the colour of their hair and their armour. To the left lay Dawn Arashiha, her dark hair matted with blood, elegant Imperial armour dented and scratched from the collapse of multiple buildings. Stirring slightly and moaning in pain. On the right lay, the still form of Riven, her snowy hair splayed out like rays of moonlight radiating from her soft face, marred only by the scar over her right eye. Her tight black leathers with their purple accents had been stripped aside to expose the puncture wounds of the arrows that had only just been removed from her body. Five witches surrounded each of the crystalline platforms. Clad in black gauzy dresses with dark filmy veils covering their faces. The witches swayed and chanted in unison, conjuring alternately dark or light globes that sprouted limbs or the visage of an imp-like creature before floating toward the women and being absorbed into their flesh, disappearing from sight.

In her tiny voice, the child inquired, "Are you really their mother? All of them?" looking up with wide innocent eyes.

The aged woman chuckled with a sound like dried leaves rustling against one another. In her rasp, she replied, "Not as you mean it child, no. It is more a title. I am the head of the witches in the Empire. Their mentor, trainer, advisor and guide. It has been mine to lead them to the paths destiny has in store for them. Mother is a term of respect and endearment for our close bond, for we are in our way, a family." Leaning down and boring into the child with her sunken eyes, "Are you truly their daughter?"

Ameliana shifted her gaze back to the wounded women, who had protected her so far and avoided the question by asking another, "Will they be alright? What's happening to them? Are those women witches too? Like Riven?"

The Mother's thin lips curled into a sly and approving smile, and her voice scratched, "They will live and rise again. And yes the women you see are witches but not like Riven. These are of our sub clan of Bone Menders, those who have talent in the healing arts or the summoning and command, of those who can knit flesh, and bone, mind and spirit of the living, or nearly so."

Looking back up at the Mother's withered face, Ameliana pressed, "Is the Black Witch a Bone Mender?"

The Mother's hissing laughter displayed no hint of annoyance at the child's questions, "Black Witch, their name for her. Fitting I suppose, and she embraced it well. Used it to her advantage, as she does with all things. No child, she has many talents but healing is one of her weaker ones. Riven is one of our more... public faces, or was before she went into hiding. She used our fearsome reputation and mystery to great advantage, and grew it more," she admitted grudgingly. "Our Coven has many sub clans, specialties as it were. Entry is based on the talent or talents of the individual witch. Riven belongs to several, the Wraith Watchers, our eyes and ears, talented in scrying and summoning watchers, the finding of lost items and people. The Sojourners, witches who enter society and take up public positions, represent the coven, and connect us to the outside. The Soul Renders, witches skilled in battle, enhancements, and the siphoning of energies from other beings. She was nearly admitted to the Whisperers, those with knowledge of names and aspects, the powers of the cosmos. Yes, she has many talents among us, but greater than that is her will. When that one sets her eyes on a task, you can be sure it will be accomplished." Her lips twisting wryly, "All save tasks regarding that one," she gestured to Dawn. "The one that changed her." The old woman's gaze was drawn to Dawn and the energy gathering around her was palpable.

Ameliana tugged at the Mother's arm, "Don't hurt her!" She cried, her voice pleading and eyes desperate.

The Mother's hollow gaze returned to her, a wicked grin exposing her yellowed teeth, "Felt that did you?" She hissed. "Good. There is talent in you. Perhaps you would like to train with us? Learn the old ways and powers?" She crooned, her voice taking on a hypnotic and seductive tone.

"No." Dawn's voice sounded cool and commanding. She sat upright on her crystal pedestal, her colour looking healthier once more. The witches surrounding her ceased their chants and folded their hands inside the drooping sleeves of their dresses, hovering near in readiness, none the less Dawn continued, "She is coming home with me."

From the other pedestal came a weak cough and the strained voice of Riven, "Don't count me out. You'd never make it as a mother on your own, I'm the responsible one remember?"

Dawn didn't need to look to see in her mind's eye, the smirk on the white maned Arashiha's face.

Chapter 8

Mother Knows Best

Dawn lay back in the steaming water of the great stone tub, sinking beneath the surface letting the fragrant waters wash clean her wounds. Riven, in a similar tub a few feet away, idly flicked at the floating healing herbs in the water sending them twirling away from her body. The waters soothed their aching muscles and drew away the pain of their wounds even as the aroma cleared their heads, sharpened their senses and invigorated them. The Mother had insisted they go straight to the baths upon completion of her healing rituals, and there was no argument to be made. In the sanctuary of the Coven of the Empire, there was a saying: 'Mother knows best'.

Dawn's face broke the surface with a splash, her dark hair clinging to her soft face as rivulets of water streamed from her nose and chin. "Oh, this feels marvellous!" She chirped in happy contentment, "Do they always add such herbs to the baths? What are these? Can we get some for the house?"

Riven smirked in quiet amusement at Dawn's delight, her eyes calculating and thoughtful, "Not always, sometimes they add… other things. It depends on whether one is being rewarded, punished, taught a lesson, being made open to teaching or, as in our case now, being healed. Very few things are done in a mundane way in this place. Everything is ritual, and full of significance. It is not always an expression of arcane power. It teaches that magic can be found in the clever application of the mundane, and it is not always pleasant. I have had snakes in the bath water, powders to induce itching, stenches rather than fragrance, food spiked with toxins to numb. Whatever was necessary to get a point across or instil the proper frame of mind, or provide a distraction to be overcome. We are being honoured now. Aided extravagantly, and I suspect buttered up for something. There will be requests to come, mark my words,". Riven stated prophetically. "And no we won't be taking any with us, what happens in the Sanctuary, stays in the sanctuary. Trade secrets I'm afraid, and we likely couldn't afford these ingredients." She smiles enigmatically. "It is nice though. Certainly, beats the salamanders that kept me company once upon a time," she laughs with a rueful face.

Dawn grimaced at some of the bath time additions, "So, everything is a lesson? Each moment crafted to instil a value of some kind or prepare one for what is to come?"

Riven nodded solemnly, "Everything, or so she says. To be honest sometimes, I am convinced she is just being intentionally mystical and letting the witches build in what meaning they may." She laughs.

Dawn nodded thoughtfully, and shot Riven a look of concern, "What do you think Ameliana is learning? Should we have let her go with them? Riven, is she in danger?" She asked half climbing out of the tub.

Riven made a soothing gesture, watching the droplets rain from Dawn's body, "She'll be fine,". She smirked. "There are rules. No one trains with the Coven unless they come willingly, and even then, there is a period of trial, ensuring the candidate has the needed discipline, and a mutual level of understanding is reached. She is getting a tour, being shown what there is to offer, but afterward, there is a required time outside. The idea is usually that the outside world will seem bland by comparison, but we live an exciting life. I think we can offer other enticements. For that one, just the offer of warmth consistency and protection may be enough. I wonder how long she has been alone," Riven mused, her voice tinged with sadness. Riven's eyes looked far away as though seeing the places she described, "From the Stella heptagonus, the Mother would have taken her to the classrooms and laboratories, to observe those in training, likely selecting opportune moments where a young witch discovers some new power. She will be shown the kitchens. Enticed by the smells of gourmet cooking and plenty. The dormitories, see that the place is comfortable, well appointed, and warm. She will see the library, and be impressed with the repository of knowledge and the promise of new worlds. The gardens, where we tend and grow exotic herbs and plants with mystical properties. She will see the scrying chambers, where witches remotely view a number of locations in crystals, and bowls of specially prepared waters, depending on the talent of the individual looking. Lastly, she will see the summoning chambers, where Daegon are brought to us and interrogated for their knowledge. There she will see power and control, and that there is nothing a witch need fear. A powerful motivator for a child who has been so very afraid." Riven nods sagely.

Dawn's face is drawn with fear and concern, the pang of loss for a child she has only just met, a feeling she knows so well. "Riven, you are not inspiring me with confidence here. It, it sounds wonderful. She'll stay with them; why would she go with us?"

Riven smirks at her, "It is wonderful, and hard. Stark and harsh realities underlie each and every marvel. She is perceptive, she will see and feel what is demanded in each scenario she sees. There is wonder and there is terror, but she will leave with us."

Looking to Riven hopefully, Dawn's voice is barely a whisper, "how do you know?"

Turning her confident gaze back to her cousin Riven replies, "Because the Black Witch already knows these wonders and can share them as well, because it is the Mother who shows her, and I know the Mother, and because I know you Dawn, and what you will offer." Riven's lips curl into a warm smile as she rises from the tub, her wounds nothing but a memory, and begins to dress.

Dawn too exits the tub her colour returned and the wicked gash in her abdomen no longer visible, "What will I off?" She began interrupted by the opening door.

Ameliana was ushered abruptly into the bathing room. The mother's stride brisk and purposeful. Mother's raspy voice was certain and commanding, "Good you are healed, it is time you took your leave. The legions are stirred by your presence and meddling; they seek you aggressively. Our Sanctum must not be discovered. You will be shown an exit and provided some escort. It was a pleasure hosting you, but for now," The Mother turned to the little girl, "Ameliana say goodbye to your friends and we will have rooms prepared for you so you can begin your training."

A stunned silence fell over the hall, Dawn looking stricken, Riven unsurprised, and Ameliana blinking in confusion, and the first to break the silence. "I. I can stay?" she asked her small voice a mixture of excitement and uncertainty, "But..." she looked at Dawn for guidance.

Her hackles up, Dawn spat back, "She will be coming with us." She declared extending a hand toward Ameliana. The girl looked confused and frightened, her gaze passing back and forth between the two women.

The Mother laughed, the sound like sandpaper scratching at roughened wood. "Don't be silly, we can take better care of her here. See to her needs and to her education, offer her a life and powers she can only dream of. You are far too busy in your city, and from what I hear from your cousin hardly one to live the example a child needs." The last earning her a knowing glare from Riven, who oddly remained silent refusing to rise to the bait. "What could you possibly offer her that is better than she could find here among us?"

Ameliana slowly turned toward the mother reaching out her hand, but Dawn grabbed her frail shoulder and spun the girl around. "Ameliana, I know this place is wonderful, and what the Mother says is true after a fashion, but the city where we live, Corillium, is no less fascinating. A place of adventure, and safety. Above ground, the buildings gleam in the sun and the trees and plants are enchanted to protect and soothe those who walk in the groves. Riven is trained in the craft and can show you things if that is what you wish, but mostly I would like to be your mother. To show you the love of a parent to a child, to raise you and help you grow." Looking abashed, "And to do a bit of growing myself. Would... would you like that do you think?"

Riven's lips curled into a knowing grin and the Mother scowled at Dawn, her gaze enough to wither the forest and freeze an ocean. Ameliana's bright smile would thaw that frost as she leapt into Dawn's arms, "Really? You mean it?" she cooed. Dawn simply nodded as a matter of factly and hugged the child close, lifting her and carrying the girl in her arms.

Riven interposed herself between her mentor and her cousin, "You can't argue with love I am afraid. After all, Mother knows best for their children." she smirked.

The Mother raised a clawed hooked hand at Riven and crooked a finger to Dawn commandingly, "You will return in a month's time and we will discuss what you owe for our aid this day, and I will hear more of your fair city."

Turning to the child, "The offer to live here and train properly," she glared at Riven, "will remain open, should you wish to better yourself child."

Cutting off Dawn's inevitable retort, the Black Witch replied rapidly, "Thank you Mother, we are most grateful for your generosity. We are ready to go and will lead the legions away from you."

Chapter 9

Legions of Streets

Bursting out into the sunlight of a new day, Dawn shields her eyes and squints, as Riven follows her out. Ameliana in her arms, glancing back at her cousin about to speak before losing her train of thought, as the passage they just came through seemingly vanishes before her eyes, "It's...gone?" she says a little astonished.

Riven smiles at Ameliana "I am glad you chose us." she says genuinely, offering a small loving smile.

Dawn looked to Ameliana, "And if you had said no I wasn't above bribing you." she teased playfully.

"What does bribing mean?" Ameliana asked with a happy but confused look.

Dawn giggled softly, "It means you can have an entire room to yourself! with lots of pillows!" Ameliana eyes widened in disbelief as she squealed in delight, "I've never had a room!" she said joyously.

Riven frowned a little and looked at Dawn, "You know our new house is almost already finished right?" She stated.

Dawn shrugged dismissively, "It's fine, she can have your room." She teased as she poked her tongue out at Riven.

Riven chuckled, "I'm sure one of the many spare bedrooms you insisted on adding will be more than perfect." she retorted, before adopting her more serious expression, as she glances back over her shoulder, "Oh that? Yes, the entrance or exits move. They never remain in the same place twice. How do you think we are all but unknown within the Celestial city, even during such a crisis as this?"

she offers as she glances up towards one of the cities towers, and the scene above, as the swirling maelstrom of Malaak, the prince of damnation tears at the fabric of creation.

Ameliana smiles back at Riven, then looks over as they all refer to the vanishing passageway making a 'oh' sound before looking back at Dawn and Riven, "We need to get off the streets before it's too dark." she says in a small voice.

Dawn nods her head and looks to Riven, "Have a plan to get us out?"

Riven sighs and shakes her head, "No I don't. I was hoping the coven would, but we are in the middle of the city, quite the spot for them to strand us." shaking her head again before looking at Dawn quizzically, "Can you not just open us a portal?"

Dawn smiled sadly and shook her head, "My magics are far to drained, and besides I'm looking quite good for a woman who was all but dead a few hours ago." she jested.

Riven nodded solemnly before passing Ameliana over to Dawn. "Here take her. I don't think I need to tell you to be careful with her?"

Dawn raises her eyebrow and looks unamused at Riven, "I would hit you, but I love you too much." she teases before looking at Ameliana, "But she is right, we need to get moving."

Riven just smirks at Dawn, for a moment before speaking, "We are all agreed there, cousin and while I don't have a plan to get us out yet. I know someone who will." Taking one last glance around to get her bearings Riven starts off sprinting ahead with Dawn and

Ameliana close behind. "We have to avoid the Legion. They are out in force. The last report I overheard on our way out was they were focusing their search, district by district starting at the Gardens, and since we are in the District of Aecius, I say we take the long way around and try to avoid the main force."

Struggling to keep up to Riven in her tight and light weight leather armour, Dawn runs as fast as she can in her robed imperial battle mage armour, holding Ameliana in her arms, "Sounds like at least some kind of plan," she offers between short sharp breaths.

Ameliana nuzzles into Dawn's neck and closes her eyes tightly as the three of them sprint through street after street, rounding bend after bend, and making several double backs at dead ends, "You promise to take me with you? You aren't going to leave me?" she says in a little-worried voice as they come to yet another dead end.

Dawn looks into Ameliana's eyes and smiles at her, with absolute adoration, "We aren't leaving you behind Ameliana, I owe you my life. You saved me, and you deserve far better than to live in this city. I said that I wanted to be your mother, and if you would have me, I would be honoured. First, we have to get all of us out of here. All or nothing?" She looks over to Riven, "Right?"

Riven nods her head in agreement, and responds, not missing a single beat or taking the time to even think of her response, as it comes naturally, "Right." Her eyes scan the street, "This shouldn't be a dead end. It wasn't when I was here last, although last time I didn't have the entire bloody city chasing me." she curses before smiling back at Dawn apologetically, "Sorry, not your fault, I know."

Dawn sighs and shakes her head, "No. It is, but we will make it out of this Riven. We always do. Besides this isn't nearly as bad as the time we got captured by the necromancer."

Riven raises her eyebrow skeptically and smirks teasingly, "Well depends on how you look at it. Instead of a maze of tunnels and caves, we are in a maze of streets and dead ends, with a threat lurking around every corner we come upon." she points out.

Dawn shrugs, "So? Last time we didn't have anything really to live for. Well we had a lot but this time." smiling warmly and looks at Ameliana, "This time, it is so much more important that we escape." pausing then adding, "and we aren't tied down onto an altar."

Riven rolls her eyes and shakes her head, "No, I suppose, we aren't but only moments ago we were near death's door." she retorts before glancing at Ameliana, taking courage in the innocent little face before nodding her head, "Right. We can't fail." Turning on her heels Riven sprints into action running up to the wall and vaulting herself up and catching onto a window seal, hauling her form up and into the window of the second story of what looks like a bakery. Riven's head pops out of the window a few moments later and holds down her arms, "Pass me Ameliana." she urges.

Dawn looks at Ameliana then back to Riven holding the child up to her cousin. Riven pulls Ameliana up and disappears inside the window again as she sets Ameliana down to the side, "Stay put. I need to get Dawn now," she offers in a warm and caring voice before looking back out the window and offering her arms down again, "Jump and I will pull you up."

Dawn jumps reaching out and grabbing hold of Riven's forearms almost yanking her out of the window with her weight, and the weight of her metal armour, "Let me go Riven. I will find another way in." she offers seeing how her cousin strains to hold her.

Riven smirks at her, "Me give up? On you? Never. Come on." she groans as she plants her legs on the wall and pulls with all her strength. Leaning her weight backward, as she draws Dawn up. As Dawn clears the window ledge, Riven's hold gives, and they both tumble backward onto the floor, sprawling across the tiles.

Riven gazes up at Dawn, "You know... if you wanted to be on top. All you need do is ask." she teases.

Dawn rolls her eyes and then rolls off Riven, "Come on, what's the plan now?" she asks as she moves over to Ameliana and picks her up again, letting the child cuddle into her again.

"Fine, be like that." Riven murmurs under her breath as she pulls herself up, "Right. Plan. Well um. This is as far as I got." she offers.

Riven peaks out the window of the bakery then look back at Dawn and Ameliana, "We will wait here for a few moments, let them pass. Then we will slip down into the sewers. I know a shortcut. Sol and I once used it when we were kids." Riven says giving a fond smile for a moment, as she seemingly looks through Dawn and Ameliana as if reliving the memory.

Dawn smiles softly at Riven, "Day dream later Riven? We have someone to save remember." Dawn teases half-heartedly before giving Ameliana a comforting squeeze.

Riven blinks for a moment and smirks at Dawn, "I have a plan now."

Raising her eyebrow, "So while you were off in your own pocket of the planes, you keep up here." Dawn mockingly taps the side of her own head, "You cultivated a grand plan did you?"

Riven smirks and holds her hands out to either side of her, "What you doubt me?"

Rolling her eyes Dawn looks to Ameliana, "You get used to her being like that, I promise." she teases before looking back to Riven, "You know very well I would follow you anywhere."

Riven laughs softly, "That's just because you want to stare at my ass when you are following me." She retorts.

Dawn looks mock offended, "Me? Never! You're my cousin, Riven." Dawn says before smiling innocently, "Although, sorry you caught me, well, you know." simply gesturing at Riven's rear, "Can't blame me, can you?"

Riven tsks playfully, "Of course I can't I'm perfect."

Dawn pouts softly, "I thought I was the perfect one."

Riven giggles softly, "You don't have the white hair, that gives me a one up on you." Walking over to Dawn, Riven pats her on the head softly, "But it's okay Dawn, you can still at least, almost be perfect." she teases.

Dawn sticks her tongue out at Riven, "Now, what is this grand plan you have thought of."

Meanwhile Ameliana has been turning her head from Riven to Dawn, to Riven, back to Dawn in utter confusion, at the ridiculous banter exchanged between the two girls, "Umm... the bad men in armour will be here soon. Can we leave?" she says in a small voice.

Riven nods her head to Ameliana, "Of course we can, now that we have my grand plan anyway."

Dawn rolls her eyes again, "Well, do you plan on sharing this plan with us anytime soon?" she asks sarcastically.

Riven simply nods, "Yep, we are going to get caught." Walking over to the window Riven spots a contingent of Legionnaires down the end of the road, waving her arms out to get their attention, "We are over here! We surrender!" she shouts at them.

Dawn's eyes go wide in fear, confusion, then anger, "Riven! What are you doing? They will kill us!" she all but shouts.

Riven looks to Dawn and offers a reassuring smile, "Do you trust me, Dawn?"
Dawn's expression becomes one of strained pain, "I... Do... but you are beginning to make me regret that Riven."

Riven kneels down in front of the trembling Ameliana that has curled up into Dawn's chest plate, "Hey, little one. It's going to be okay. They aren't going to hurt us. They would never hurt the sister of Legate Sol Arashiha." she says honestly.

Dawn just looks at Riven blinking blankly, "Your brother! You are going to get us captured by your brother?"

Riven gives Ameliana a warm and reassuring hug, before looking back to Dawn and nodding her head, "I am, trust me, Dawn. I promise no harm will come to either of you."

Chapter 10

Old Friend and Family

The rough fibrous rope chafed at the wrists of the prisoners, causing Ameliana to squirm in discomfort. As they were escorted to the ruin of a former administration building in the Imperial District, they were surprised to find that the inside had been thoroughly cleaned and restored, floors polished to a high sheen, and every speck of dust rigorously and meticulously scrubbed away. Flanked by vigilant Legionnaires, standing stiff and straight backed eyeing their prisoners warily, the trio were lead to a waiting room adjoining the Legates office. The air was pregnant with tension as the Legate expressed his extreme displeasure with the message delivered by the now cowering messenger. "Arcturus Killed! In a duel!? The idiot had orders to engage a rebel city not a single man, I don't care who this... Kratus is or used to be." At the mention of the name Dawn and Riven exchanged a look, while Ameliana sought solace in Dawn's skirts, burying her tear streaked face.

The legate continued his rage, "Who now leads the 17th then?" He demanded. The messenger stammered his curt reply, "Senior Tribune Eliana Nato had taken command when I was dispatched, sir."

The legate guffawed, "That bitch!? She hasn't the capacity to take a city such as we have been advised this one is. Confound those rebels! She will need to be kept in line... you will return at once and summon her back, no! Belay that. You will take this message..." The sound of a chair scraping the floor indicates he is sitting and writing orders, "To the Death Cult representative." a moment passes as he writes and murmurs, "Perhaps they can find the strength to deal with this... Corillium. Another debacle with these rebels, first my Mage Legion is scattered, now the 17th... I should not be surprised; the Black Witch was thrice as formidable at Legate Curo... Where in oblivion did she get to?" He murmurs venting his anger with an armoured fist pounding into the ornately carved desk.

"You could try asking her instead of making her wait in the lobby," Riven comments off handily from the waiting room. A silence ensued for a few moments, followed by the scraping of the chair once more and the clack of the Legates sabatons on the polished marble floor as he approached the door peering into the hall.

Slapping the message into the hands of the messenger, he barked, "The time to deliver this would be now, idiot! Why are you still here?" As the messenger scrambled from the room, the legate commanded, "Bring them inside.... and cut their bonds, why is she bound? Are you all insane? You're lucky she hasn't turned you all into slime filled char."

The trio is ushered into the legate's office and their bonds hurriedly cut. Ameliana hiding behind the women as the Legates six-foot frame in fighting trim stood at a menacing attention. His silver eyes cast a cold penetrating stare regarding Riven beneath his perfectly trimmed black hair cut short in military fashion. His features would be considered handsome were it not for the stern expression perpetually affixed to his visage, souring the effect slightly. As they are freed, he snaps at the Legionnaires, "Leave us." Incredulous, they begin to protest earning his withering gaze under which they wilt like fragile flowers in the desert sun. "Shut the door", he commands as the last exits, his eyes boring into Riven who seems unphased. "You have a lot of explaining to do Sister. Where have you been? And who is-" he cuts off, recognition dawning at the rather familiar features of what would appear to be Riven's twin save for the hair. "Cousin Luna?" he asks perplexed.

Dawn grins at him, a flirtatious quip ready at her lips but Riven raises a forestalling hand, speaking in her stead. "Our cousin yes, but not Luna. Legate Sol Arashiha, meet your well-named cousin Dawn. Her breaking light has changed the context of everything in recent days. Shedding light on the fact that much of what we thought we knew of the rebel empire was... incomplete at best, outright wrong might be more appropriate."

Confusion contorts his features as he looks back and forth between them. Dawn smiles brightly taking his hand, "Hello. I believe the words you are seeking are something to the effect of, 'Greetings dear cousin, your beauty enlivens the dreariness of existence, welcome to the Celestial city, how may I make your stay more comfortable?" she greets him.

Blinking at her bold words, he finds he cannot help but smile, raising her hand to his lips kissing it formally, "The gods show their mischievous side. There are two of them? Where is my willow bark I feel a headache coming on already..."

Tsking softly Dawn shakes her head and looks over to Riven as if Sol wasn't there, "You know, for a moment there, I thought I might like him, but he can be quite a buzz kill." Reaching into her bag and rummaging around for a few moments before she produces the willow bark as requested, "Here you go, do you need me or Riven to show you how to use it? Or can you handle it by yourself?" She says teasingly in a mocking tone.

Riven grins at her, "You can see that with his personality he often has to... handle it himself." she teases.

Dawn silently gasps in response to Riven's statement giving Sol a look as if to say you poor thing. Reaching forward and gently patting him on the shoulder, "There, there I am sure there is a nice lady for you in this city." Pauses and thinks for a moment, "Well maybe not just now, I'm underwhelmed with what your allies have done with the place," she shrugs and then pauses looking at Riven, "oh... That's not what you meant by handle himself did you." Smiles innocently and turns around and walks off to one side of the office whistling to herself.

Grinning impishly at her brother, "Now then, we'll need some assistance getting out of the city. It would be greatly appreciated if I didn't have to keep subduing your ill trained troops, they are becoming rather tedious."

Rising through the ranks to become the youngest legate in recent history required playing several moves ahead of others. In all the years of their sibling rivalry and competition, there were few times Riven had been treated to such a look of astonishment from her usually so well prepared brother. "What nonsense is this?" he sputtered. "Palatine Riven Arashiha you will give your report and an account of your whereabouts these last months."

"I prefer my witch title thank you very much brother." she corrects.

Sol glares at Riven with an icey intensity, his jaw grinding slowly in a moment of unusual frustration only his sister could stir within him.

Riven waved him off, "Apologies brother, we are on a tight timetable, and your men have detained us overmuch as it is. Now, kindly consult your maps and show us the quickest route from the city with passes of safe conduct. Reports will have to wait until this young lady is safely ensconced in her new home."

At last turning, his gaze upon Ameliana, causing her to cower behind Riven. "Who is this child? Why is she so important? What are you up to Riven?" He demands the questions coming rapid fire.

Remaining cool, Riven places a reassuring hand on Ameliana, "I am sorry that is Coven business brother." She bluffs, "Unless you wish to meddle in their affairs, but then you know what happened, the last time you tried to pry into their goings on." Narrowing her eyes threateningly, "And the word you're looking for is witches. With a W. Do remember impressionable young ears are present."

Sol Arashiha clenched his strong jaw. He had not risen so far so fast by being imprudent, and he knew when he was bested. The witches were unpredictable but made better allies than enemies, so it was time to change tack, and wrest what he could from his infuriating sister.

"So you are engaged on a mission for the coven? Superseding your orders from me? From the Regency? Where is your Mage legion?" He demands.

Cursing his intractability, but hardly surprised by it Riven fought to remain cool under his scrutiny, playing out the dangerous game she had engaged them in. "The Regent is not so well respected outside the chain of command here. The Dark Elves, the Nordic people's, the rest of the Empire are not looking for rescue from us, they prepare to invade and take over. To cleanse the land from the invading forces of Damnation that have destroyed, not solidified our home. Look at Amol, look at Terrelia. Look at the Capitol city here brother, in ruins, in flames. The policies of our leaders have not inspired a fear of respect, but fear to spark the need to protect themselves from the same fate. Do you remember Lady Erissia Octavius? Her brilliant plans to inspire fear in others that lead to her stretching on the end of a rope? It was nearly a disaster for us. Had we not distanced ourselves, been sceptical of her plans we may have been dragged down with her. It is scepticism and exploring wider options that lead us to rise. Such is the case now. Be open... And trust me." She implores.

Deep creases from in Sol's brow as she speaks, his knuckles turning white as he clenches his fists. His retort is biting, "This from the one who chose the path of Daegonic magic to get ahead? You of all people embrace the great plan of our people personally. Riven your words smack of treason!"

The ghost of a smile traces her lips, she had him on the right track, time to invoke the misunderstandings of her witchcraft that carried her career forward. This was familiar ground. "Exactly why you must trust me brother dear. The Coven knows the Daegon, their types and their ways, their motivations. We use the Daegon, control them and do not reach too high. The Coven fears that the Regent and her family may be more puppets than allies, who is truly in charge? We must be cautious."

"You are becoming corrupted by voices outside sister, I cannot allow you to leave again." Sol states firmly.

Dawn gave Riven a look to ask 'are you crazy? You are pushing too hard'. She clung to Ameliana protectively and began looking around the office for something to club her powerful male cousin over the head with if they had to make an escape.

Riven's reply came readily, the gambit hinging on this play, "Our knowledge of the world outside is incomplete brother. You need a set of trusted ears to learn the many versions of truth we are not told. I am shocked at how little we know."

Gesturing to Dawn. "Our own family for instance. How could we not know of an entire cousin? She, and this girl, they are keys to the future survival and dominance of our family. Proof that our knowledge needs expanding. You are not a fool brother, never have been".

Dawn beamed as she was mentioned and quickly added, "And I am quite a sight to behold! Not knowing of me is... is... umm, like not knowing who the emperor is!" she chimed before smiling innocently as she caught an eyeful from Riven.

Riven looked back at Sol stroking his ego. "Send us on our way and to further glory for our family."

With a heavy sigh, he settled back into his immaculate desk and dipped his quill, his flowing script producing passes of safe conduct and orders for an escort to the city's edge. "Hurry back Riven. My spy network suffers under the current commander, what is an empire to do without Arashiha's to show them the way hmm?" he smiles with a pride bordering on arrogance.

* * *

Outside the office, the trio is marched through the fallen streets with a guard of honour surrounding them. The once proud buildings on either side of the Cobble street become crumbling imperial architecture, empty and devoid of life like bleached skulls in desert sands, their crumbling facades like yawning maws into a heart of darkness. The mordant surroundings fitting of a city overrun by Daegon.

Dawn leans toward Riven whispering, "So how close did you bring us to getting killed or captured?"

Riven smirks at her, "What? Did you want to live forever? Umm... Pretty damn close. I wasn't sure he would buy some of that. I suppose years of lying to each other while setting each other up for success and protecting one another has paid off. I feel a bit guilty though... Still, I may have planted a few worms in his brain. If he look closely enough, he may start to realise who and what he serves."

Dawn nods thoughtfully, "But you did it. You came through."

Looking at her cousin and closest comrade, then to the child between them she nods, "The stakes were too high to lose." Even as they began to relax, Ameliana stiffened clinging tightly to their legs. Instantly alert both women scanned ahead, noting the source of Ameliana's fear. Barring the street before loomed the menacing form of an eight-foot tall demonic creature, short twisted horns rising from the mottled red and black flesh curled into a terrifying sneer.

"Ahz nazsh kugoralum... What passes here in the realm of the damned?" Its voice echoed itself as though three or more separate voices were speaking in unison.

Ameliana whimpered at the sound tears streaming down her cheeks causing Dawn and Riven to look at one another, an anger welling within both of them that this abomination would threaten the peace they sought for the little girl.

Fearfully, one of the legionnaires steps forward raising the legates pass in a shaking fist to find two feminine hands on his pauldrons pulling him back. Dawn and Riven grin at each other, their eyes holding a rapid conversation as to who would address the fiend on behalf of their party.

Dawn nodded slightly and put a comforting arm around the legions finest, leading him away, "There, there dear, stand down, you are out ranked and out classed, this is women's work." She adds an affectionate pat to his rear accompanied by an appreciative glance at the warriors form, the flirtatious gesture disarming the fear the

Daegon was accustomed to inspire. The fiend turned its incredulous attention to the snapping fingers of the white haired, scowling witch.

"That's right focus on the threat." She shakes her head as though ashamed for the hulking demonic beast. "It's a wonder your kind can hold this city, I Suppose being immortal and having a return gateway right where you re-spawn has its advantages, a do-over for every mistake." She rolls her eyes. Turning a withering gaze upon the fearsome horned visage, "Listen closely, we are trying to establish a positive bedtime routine for the child now in our care and you are upsetting our schedule. If you think a tired child can be cranky, you haven't seen me when I get annoyed. In the next two minutes, one of two things will happen, either you will stand aside and let us pass ordering all your minions to clear our path, or you will know suffering and pain as I invoke your name and make your initiation to my service a nightmare greater than your mommy demon experienced with your daddy when you were spawned. If you even think for a second to challenge me with the admittedly true fact that your kind is not made as mine is, I will revoke the two minutes and go to work on you now." Her words fire rapidly at the Daegon whose visage twists and contorts in the clearly unfamiliar expressions of bewildered confusion. It's jaw working and the flames that pass for eyes flaring to a roaring inferno. Before it can form words for its counter threat Riven gives it a look of disgust and snaps her fingers to the side, a shimmering and wavering in the air revealing the twisted reptilian forms of a pair of lesser Daegon that have been Riven's accompanying companions all along, "Minions explain!" She barks the command eyes not leaving the Greater Daegon's, as her fingers brought forth an intricately designed witches fetish.

If one were fluent in the black speech, one might be impressed by the impassioned plea of Riven's minions assuring her list of true names is long and her command of magic's strong and terrifying to be subject to. So convincing were they that the greater fiend was given pause.

At length it swept its arm wide, trailing dark flames, "Enough!" It roared drawing itself regally to its eight-foot height and giving Riven it's most commanding stare. "You are not the only one with tasks to attend to, and these childish games waste my time. Be gone from here lying witch but know your threats only serve to annoy me. Should you pass this way again, I will show you why we rule this city, and soon your pathetic world." His speech is halting, uncertain, a bravado belied by the rapid flickering of the diminished flame like eyes.

With a knowing smirk Riven waves a hand toward her minions cloaking them from sight once more and waves her party forward. "Right choice." She returns, "Let us be gone from this place." Taking rapid strides, the Legionnaires are forced to hurry to catch up and Dawn sweeps Ameliana into her arms using her longer legs to keep pace with her cousin. As they exit the flaming ruin of the Empire's heart several blocks later Dawn's curiosity gets the better of her.

"So, did you really have that one's name?" She asks.

Riven smiles wickedly, "Not yet. Would have been a terrible battle. Might be one worth seeking though. Something that powerful has its uses. If it can be controlled. That would be a battle of wills only to be tried in most dire of circumstances. Let's not do that again, shall we? But you were brilliant; your coolness in pressure was very convincing. Though the Legionnaire was kind of cute." They laugh away the tension of the city as they make their way to safety.

Chapter 11

Fresh Air

Looking around the outside of the city at the much greener grass Dawn falls forward as if she were collapsing only to twist mid-air and land on her back and sprawls out and gazes up at the somewhat dull looking sky, inhaling deeply before letting out a long sigh, "It's... Nice not to have the smell of burning, rotting, and decaying flesh filling my nostrils." She says before looking over to Riven.

Still holding Ameliana in her arms Riven is caught in the act of pulling a rather childish face at Ameliana, quickly smiling innocently at Dawn, "You saw nothing, I am the great and powerful Black Witch, that is what all of my brother's Legionnaires think and that's how it's going to stay." Nods her head rather decisively.

Dawn and Ameliana simultaneously begin laughing hysterically, after a few moments and a bit of time to regain her train of more... Mature line of thinking Dawn sits up and rolls her shoulders, "You know, I bet my fiancé will start to worry soon..." Pauses then adds, "Well, for a good reason, I did leave in the middle of the night, and we have been gone for what? 2? 3? 4? Days now." Shrugs, "I lost track."

Riven shakes her head, "And you are lucky you left the note you did, otherwise we might not be going home with this adorable little thing." She says in a childish tone to Ameliana to which Ameliana just beams happily at Riven and hugs her tightly.

Dawn grumbles something about feeling unloved before pushing herself back up onto her feet, "Well, at least neither of you were run through with a sword." She retorts and turns crossing her arms.

Riven whispers something to Ameliana before turning her head slightly to listen to Ameliana's response after a moment and a silent muffled little giggle from the pair they both nod their heads and silently sneak up behind Dawn before tackling her to the ground and hugging her, "Don't be like that, after all... If I hadn't followed you and saved you, I couldn't tell you I told you so." Riven says with a huge teasing grin on her face.

Dawn squawks as she falls forward and finds Riven and Ameliana clinging to her and holding her down, "No fair this is two on one!" She complains before laughing for a few moments her smile quickly fading from her face at the 'I told you so' from Riven. "You just had to go and say it didn't you." Dawn groans before looking back over her shoulder at Ameliana, "You watch Ameliana, we will be old and grey, and you will have kids of your own, and they will have kids! And she still wouldn't have let that one go."

Ameliana looks confused her gazes shifting between Riven and Dawn, "B-but... I am only 5?" She says a bit lost at the turn in conversation.

Riven simply smirked knowingly at Dawn, as if to say 'You know it.' After making sure Dawn gets the point before she rolls off Dawn and picks Ameliana up propping her up in her arms, "So missy, do you have a last name?" She asks curiously.

Ameliana giggles softly as she is picked up and propped up smiling happily before her expression seemingly freezes for a few moments then she frowns in deep thought for a while, "I... Uh... I don't remember." She murmurs quietly, "I..." She begins to tear up a little as she becomes choked for words.

Riven coos soothingly to her and holds her closely, "It's okay Ameliana, it's alright... I know it must be hard... It's just I wanted to make sure."

Dawn hearing Ameliana's turn in emotional state moves up onto her knees and shuffles over smiling warmly at Ameliana and gently moving her hair out of the child's face, "Ameliana, I... I mean we couldn't even imagine knowing what you went through while you were on your own... how hard it must have been to not remember your last name." Pauses for a few moments, "It's funny in a way I came here looking for my own last name, and instead I found you." She smiles and looks over to Riven.

Riven nods her head encouragingly, "And, well, I think I can finish for Dawn here, is... That if you want you can share the same last name she and I use." Smiling brightly, "So, what do you say, Ameliana Arashiha?"

Ameliana listens quietly while rubbing her teary eyes before she slowly comes out of hiding as she is coaxed by Dawn then looks to Riven as she speaks, her expression slowly brightening until the very last words Riven speaks. "Yes!" She squeals joyously as she wraps her arms around Riven.

Dawn pouts a bit, "Aww no hug for me?" She whines playfully.

Ameliana rolls her eyes slightly and reaches over grabbing at Dawn's hand and pulling her over, "My arms are only small." Ameliana offers as an explanation for Dawn being left out of the hug. Dawn hugs Ameliana and Riven tightly, then laughs, "I know little one."

Riven smirks slightly, "It's okay Ameliana Arashiha, take no notice of Dawn, she just likes to complain a lot." She teases.

Dawn shakes her head at Riven as she steps back, "Hey, I am meant to be the mature one, I don't complain." She protests and pokes her tongue out at Riven.

In unison Riven and Ameliana roll their eyes and shake their heads, "No, you're not." They say together before looking at each other and giggling softly.

Ameliana smiles happily as they all begin to walk away from the ruined city, "So, what happens now?" She asks in a soft voice.

Dawn smiles softly at her as she responds, "We go home little one, we go home."

Epilogue

The stars glittered invitingly in the clear cool night sky, their pinpoint lights speaking of mysterious origins and primal language to the Celestial power in Dawn, the same pull inside of her that had drawn her to want to study the stars. The choking smoke and red tinged glow of the flames from the city behind them. It was almost as if they had entered another world, albeit a more peaceful one. The trio walked down the road, eager to put distance between themselves and memories best left behind, but after a time, their steps became more and more a leaden trudging. Something within her interpreted the light of the heavens, reading the sky like a map, Dawn lead them from road to path, ever away from the city but along less well-travelled paths and eventually into the countryside.

Riven watched her curiously but trusted the confidence she saw in her cousin's demeanour. "We should find a place to rest for the night. We can divide the watch between us Dawn but this little one is almost asleep on her feet."

"Mhm," Ameliana murmurs sleepily.

Dawn waves her hand at them, "We are almost there."

"There?" Riven inquires suspiciously, "What is there?

Her face splitting into a proud grin, "There!" Dawn points through the trees where they could spy a small clearing with some sort of stone structure. An eerie glow emanated from the structure ahead, its pale blue light only visible due to the darkness of the night and the obscuring shadows. Were it daylight the entire structure would have been very difficult to see at all.

Riven stares incredulous, "What is this place? How did you know it was here?"

Dawn just shrugs, "It's where we needed to go, C'mon it's late, and I am tired." She presses forward hoping to head off further questions.

The structure was ancient and heavily ruined, but their examination showed that it was made of a very dense and dark grey-green stone, cut into impossibly large sections. The tight fitting seams were only visible at all due to the weathering and age. In its day, the structure must have appeared to have been of one piece of stone. The precision masonry was exquisite, including intricate archways of stone latticework, though now in ruins with pieces missing the artistry and complexity was not lost upon the weary adventurers.

Dawn pats Riven's leather clad arm, "Thank you for volunteering for the first watch. Very gracious of you."

About to protest, Riven just shrugs, someone had to take first watch, she would just have to sit somewhere very uncomfortable to keep awake. She nods her assent, "It's defensible enough and above all close. Meets my criteria."

Riven and Dawn scoops up piles of evergreen needles and spread a cloak over them making a surprisingly inviting bed. Their efforts reveal the source of the soft glow; the floor was decorated with a large slab of polished dark marble at least two meters on a side. Embedded into the marble were crystalline structures, enchanted to collect and redistribute the light of the moon and stars. Dawn gasped in awe as she realised there was a pattern to their inlay and looked up to the heavens to confirm her suspicions.

"It's the stars directly overhead! This location as mapped by the heavens. No wonder I knew where to come." Dawn grins impishly. "This ruin must have been built by the Prima, the first peoples from whom the elves are descended. According to legend anyway. It is said the Prima built the first incarnation of the Celestial city we just left. The architecture certainly matches the towers there but the stone here is darker."

Riven shakes her head in wonder, "I would ask how you were able to guide us here but you might need to explain it. Another time when my mind is not so foggy." She hugs Ameliana and kisses her forehead, "Goodnight little one, I'll be watching over you as you sleep."

Laying on the makeshift bed of cloak covered with pine needles, Dawn holds out her arms to the little girl and invites her in, cuddling the child to a nearly instantaneous slumber. Riven's lips curl into a contented grin as she divides her attention between watching them sleep and scanning their surroundings. With time and inaction, however, came a series of thoughts, and with thoughts, questions. Questions she resolved to ask when Dawn awoke.

The wait was a quiet one, fortunately, for Riven had to question if she could so much as lift her bow due to the exhaustion of their trials and travel. Her tired eyes caught a glint of something reflecting the strange pulsing light of the crystals. Forcing her tired muscles to the motion, she padded over to the corner and began to clear more of the brush away.

The decayed mush of what was likely once a wooden chest. Part of the detritus has slid away from the contents of the forgotten vessel revealing an ingot of silvery metal. Curious she tried to lift it but nearly fell backward as it was far lighter than expected. "What in the world?" She whispered, settling her stance and applying more control.

Over the course of her watch, she managed to clean the shining metallic bar and make it ready for travel. Soon it was at last time to wake her cousin. Reluctant to disturb her Fa'en like form, she gently shook her awake automatically leaning back out of the way to avoid the anticipated slapping away.

"Shhh, shhh, don't wake the child, it's your watch but we should talk a moment first." Riven whispers.

Dawn's non-committal grunt served as agreement enough, it seemed for she started to crawl forth issuing a glare to Riven for waking her as she covered Ameliana with the cloak. "You were supposed to watch for more than ten minutes before my turn and don't try to convince me that it's been hours, I am on to your tricks witch." she teases.

Riven chuckled quietly, knowing better than to argue with something so paltry as the truth. Instead, her face grew serious, regarding Dawn with her silver eyed stare, "Dawn, why did you choose the middle of the night to slink away to the most dangerous part of the old empire? What were you doing in the city?"

Unprepared for the question she tries to make a quip but her tired brain conjures nothing, leaving her only with the truth. "I went looking for my past. My heritage. I was nosing about through my tutor's home and one of lady Valeriana's journals happened to fall open. I came across some notes that referred to my father, and the circumstances as to how he and my mother met. The real one, not the wonderful one who raised me. I had a name and the stories... granted most of those were rather unflattering but... I wanted to know more. Who was this Gaius Sabinus, what other family might have been there? What did he do? Where did he live? Other than the man, who impregnated my mother, his..." she sighs heavily shaking her head. "I just wanted to know myself, who I am." she confessed.

Riven threw her arms around her dark haired cousin hugging her tightly, "Damn that woman and her schemes. Still, I can't fault any plan that leads to you," She admits grudgingly. "Dawn, my River, my cousin, you know who you are. The blood in your veins is foremost yours before any connection to your progenitors can be claimed. You make your own decisions, you make your destiny, and you choose your path. You are the aptly named Dawn, the light of our lives, the hope of the morning that keeps the rest of us who are privileged to know you strong. But you must know that we are stronger together. Better in tandem. Look at us, we have fought through and survived by fighting at each other's side, for each other. It was foolish to go off alone. You have nothing to hide from me, nor any judgement to fear. Whatever your heritage you are you now, and you are not alone." she looks pleadingly to her cousin, "I would have come with you in a heartbeat," her sly grin appears, "It would have been a lot easier than tracking you across two counties. Fortunately, no one can hide from a Wraith watcher, certainly not one as determined as I. I might have been a little worried." Riven shuffles her foot.

"Aww, you do care," Dawn smirked. "I am sorry, I know you do and I really shouldn't have left without you. I realized it even when I went unconscious. Riven, good as I am, you are right. We are better together. I won't wander off on my own again, at least not without telling you. Certainly, not tonight while I am on watch. Go get some sleep you." she nudges her cousin toward the makeshift bed, "And keep our daughter warm."

Their daughter. The thought struck home more deeply still. How were they going to raise a child? Two women prone to adventure and danger now needing to be models of responsibility? Riven shrugged once more, the thoughts would wait for the morning.

Settling in, Dawn finally noticed the strange metallic lump, "Riven! Where did you find this?" She squeals in an excited whisper.

Tiredly, Riven points to the corner and oblivious to Dawn's excitement drifts to a deep sleep. Dawn, however, had found just the thing to keep her awake. Star metal. Created by the Prima, the art of making the incredibly strong yet lightweight alloy had been lost for millennia. She admired the ingot for a time, wondering at the sparkling filaments that seemed to flow throughout, trying to divine its make like so many before her, had if it were a mixture of materials or a property of the crystalline structure. Here was a lump of it, just waiting for them in the wilds, found on the same trip as their daughter. It could not be a coincidence. Dawn resolved that their daughter would one day benefit from this priceless find.

* * *

"You Know I'm going to miss the Celestial City." Chimed Dawn.

The pair stopped to take one last look at the now distant Celestial City almost glimpsing the beauty, the once great city must have possessed in days long since the past.

Riven raised her brow questioningly, "I somehow doubt that…" she said skeptically.

Dawn nodded a few times, "True, true but just think about all the greenery and life of Corillium and the Protectors Forest. Surely, the Wood Elves must get sick of looking at their Woodland Realm, day in day out." She teased.

Riven giggled as she shook her snowy mane, "Of course that's what you would complain about." she retorted.

Dawn gasped in shock, "Didn't I tell you that I don't complain?" she retorted before giggling herself softly, "But in all truth, one thing I will miss is the adventures."

Riven shook her head at Dawn as she spoke starting in a sincere but serious tone, "We have just volunteered to become mothers, and you are engaged, and you are a mage, and I am a Witch… what kind of adventure do you want!" she offered ending in a teasing tone.

Dawn shrugged a little, "Oh who knows, maybe a war or an ancient ruin. something new." she jested.

Riven shook her head once more, "How about long-winded Senate speeches, or worse political study."

Dawn puffed her chest out proudly, "Huh! just because I'm the Consul of the Haven of Naernay." she teased, "I am the best diplomat in the entire Empire." she joked.

Rolling her eyes Riven glanced down to check on the sleeping form of Ameliana, "I'm sure between the lot of us Arashiha we might come close to starting a dynasty of Consuls and diplomats of Corillium."

Dawn smirked, "Although the Count and Countess might have something to say to that, you know what people say about a Lyeis and their silver tongues."

Ameliana stirred in her sleep before looking up at the two, "What's a Lyeis?" she cooed in a sleepy tone.

Dawn giggled softly as she paused to peek down at Ameliana, "Don't worry about them, you will meet them soon enough little one, after all, they are part of your new family as well." she chimed cheerfully.

Riven smiled fondly before looking out over the near horizon towards the border of the Capital County and Aquielia, "Remind me to bring horses next time." she said flatly as the sheer distance ahead of them becomes all too apparent.

Smiling innocently Dawn nudges Riven, "Bring Horses next time." she teased before side stepping to avoid the inevitable swipe of Riven's hand only missing her by mere millimeters.

The End

The Chronicles of Corillium

The Haven of Naernay

Authors

Daniel J. Breen and Tristram Ross

Book II

Chapter 1

Home Sweet Home

Laying out in the afternoon sun, Dawn was dozing happily to the sounds of the little girl, Ameliana, chasing her other mother, Riven, around the courtyard. The five-year-old girl dances merrily around the lounges, her auburn hair bouncing with each skipping step and her amber eyes alight with glee as the snowy-maned Riven lunges and spins in her dark purple and black leathers attempting to scoop the child into her arms, her grey eyes full of loving mirth.

Dawn brushes her unruly brown hair from her face, the intricate bracelet of woven platinum bejeweled to depict the constellations above the continent of Fa'aell catching the light and causing Riven to smile.

Dawn turned slightly, and looked off to one side before waving over one of the servants, beckoning them closer, "Could you go and get my fiancé for me please?" she asks.

The timid female servant clothed in a white short dress bows her head, dark curls bobbing, "I am sorry to inform you but your fiancé is off on business."

Dawn sits up suddenly in alarm, "When did he leave? How long is he going to be gone for?" she asks in a barrage of questions.

Stammering over her words the petite girl wilts a little, "Ah... I am not sure my lady, he didn't tell me, I had assumed he talked to you." she says in an apologetic tone not daring to move lest she is scolded.

Dawn smiles comfortingly at her, "It's fine, it's not your fault, but I suppose fair is only fair." she chimes happily as she looks over to Riven and Ameliana, "My lovely childish girls, I don't suppose you two are up for a trip?" Dawn says, a devious little smile curling across her lips, countering any menace to the scar that crosses her right eye, as an idea comes to mind.

Ameliana stops chasing Riven and looks over to Dawn, wearing a delicate petite dress her hair tied into a little bun as she beams over at her, "That sounds like fun!" she chimes happily.

Riven paused, noticing she is no longer the target of Ameliana's attention, walks over and scoops her up, wandering over to sit down beside Dawn, "Look at our little girl, all ready for adventure." she tsks softly shaking her head, "We will make an Arashiha out of you yet little one." she teases.

Ameliana looks confused for a time turning from Dawn to Riven, "I thought I was an Arashiha." she says with a little pout.

Dawn kisses Ameliana's cheek, "You are! What Riven meant to say, is that Arashiha women are somewhat known for their flair, as it were." she says with a little teasing grin glancing to Riven with a knowing look.

Laughing softly, Riven nods her head, "Mhm that we are, which is why so many people drool over Dawn despite her being engaged, and why lots of people fear me as the black b--, err witch, with a W." she says with a funny smile as she looks back to Dawn.

Ameliana puffs her little chest out a bit, "And me! For being me!" she chimes as well beaming at her two mothers, eliciting agreeing nods from both, "So, where are we going?" She pauses then quickly adds, "Please not back to the big scary city," referring to the Celestial City, the capital of the empire now overrun with demonic Daegon and in ruins. Ameliana had somehow managed to survive there for some time before Dawn and Riven rescued her and brought the little girl home.

In unison, Dawn and Riven, both add, "Don't worry we won't." Giving Ameliana a little pat on the head, "Alright, so we will go home." Dawn proclaims.
"Aren't we already home?" Ameliana asks confused further as she looks around the large Country House they all share, the courtyard flanked by arched walkways that lead back into the spacious interior of their Corillium home.

"Well, yes, we are home, but home is where the heart is." she chimes giving Ameliana's little chest a poke, "Right here, and that means, we are at home when we are all together." Dawn paused for a moment and blinks, "Well huh, when did I get so sappy." she asks a little confused.

Riven smirks, "Well, we did get a daughter, and you are getting married." Riven says and pokes Dawn's side, "You're getting soft." she teases.

Rolling her eyes, "Right. Me? Get soft? Never!" Dawn retorts before adding, "Oh and we are going to the Arashiha estate, so you can learn about our family heritage."

Riven laughs softly, "I think that might be a learning experience for us all."

Dawn nods her head, "Mhm, that's the point, although for this little one and me." she teases smiling warmly at Ameliana, "After all, you are a full Arashiha." Dawn points out, "So, you shall be our mentor, oh great, powerful and wise Snowy Manned Arashiha." Dawn jests whilst mockingly bowing to Riven.

Ameliana rolls her eyes at the pair of them, "Calm down you two. Otherwise, people might think I am the adult here." she teases.

Dawn and Riven blink and laugh in unison, "Why would they think that?" they both tease playfully.

"So, when do we leave?" the little girl asks looking at the two goofs that pose as her mothers.

Dawn purses her lips for a few moments, "hmm, well, I suppose we could leave in a few days, after all, Riven is very important in the Senate at the moment, so we need to give at least some notice."

Riven shakes her head, "It might take some more doing than that dear Dawn, I'm not sure how much anyone will like the city Consul taking vacation days." she teases.

Ameliana pouts softly, "B-but I wanted to go now." she whines softly as she snuggles into Riven.

Dawn smiles sympathetically, "Well, I am afraid that's impossible, besides it's time for your nap."

"I'm not tired." she retorts before poking her tongue out at Dawn.

Dawn gasps softly in mock offence. "She gets that sass from her mother you know." Dawn scolds playfully before looking at Ameliana again, "Besides, you may not be tired, but I am."

"But weren't you sleeping only a few moments ago?" asks the little voice, with a curious air about it.

Dawn screws up her face, "Well yes. Uh, well, Riven and I have business to attend to, so off to bed with you little one." patting Ameliana's bottom and then gesturing with her head to Riven.

Riven gives Dawn a knowing smirk, "Come on Ameliana, we don't want you getting all tired and cranky like Dawn." she teases, standing up and beginning to walk towards the open doors.

Dawn glares at Riven for a time, "I heard that!" she calls after the pair.

"Who said you weren't meant to?" Riven responds with a little snicker as she looks down at Ameliana and winks.

They walked into the spacious light coloured interior, marble walls and pillars supporting the room, various pieces of art, ranging from paintings to statues and other unusual niceties dotted the room. Heading forward to a door that leads to another room where the decorum changes to a homier feel. There was less intruding sunlight, but the room glowed from the candles. In the hearth of the marble fireplace, a fire danced. The flickering of the firelight sent corresponding shimmers throughout the room making the shadows appear to dance in time. Two chairs and a bench sat in front to capture the warmth as well as a large wolf fur rug where Ameliana loved to sprawl. The small windows in the room were covered with glass and shutters, keeping any prying eyes as well as the elements out. Heading to a spiral staircase, Riven takes a quick look around the interior and lets out a little sigh, as a flood of memories flows through her mind.

Ameliana tugs on Riven's arm, "What are you thinking about?" the small voice asks curiously.

Blinking back to reality, Riven looks down at Ameliana in her arms, "Oh, nothing, just something Dawn said earlier. Besides, it's not something you need to know until you are much, much older." Riven states rather firmly.

Ameliana screws her face up a bit, "Meanie." she huffs before turning her head away from Riven.

Tsking softly, Riven begins to walk up the stairs, "Come on little one, don't be like that. You know the deal, we pretend to be the adults because we know the adult stuff, and you get to be the carefree child we spoil with lots and lots of love!" she chimes before nuzzling Ameliana playfully then blowing a raspberry on her little belly, causing her to start giggling hysterically.

Coming to the top of the stairs, Riven waltzes into Ameliana's new room, "You know, this room is twice the size of mine, when I was your age." Riven says with a little nod, sitting down on the end of the bed and tucking Ameliana in.

"Really?" Ameliana asks softly as she looks around her room with a renewed awe.

"Mhm, you are very lucky little one, and you should never forget that. None of us should. You have people that love you, and we ourselves are fortunate to be rather well off, and some of the most powerful women in all the Empire." Kissing Ameliana's cheek, "Never let our privilege go to your head, after all not all of us out there were lucky enough to have a silly woman that goes around calling herself Dawn, come and rescue us." she chuckles nuzzling Ameliana once more before she finishes tucking her in.

"That is something we both have in common," she states wistfully raising to her feet and moving the lit candle to the far side of the room. "Sleep well little one," she calls out, creeping out the door and closing it behind her.

Resting her back against it Riven glances up at the ceiling, "Not many of us are so fortunate," she repeats to herself before taking a deep breath, "Damn being a parents is much tougher than I had thought." shaking her head and laughing to herself as she makes her way back downstairs in search of Dawn.

Meanwhile, Ameliana just looks at the door in confusion at what just happened. Looking around her room once more before she settles down, "Love you too mummy." she whispers softly, rolling over and closing her little eyes.

Sitting downstairs by the fire, a glass of wine in her hand Dawn looks over her shoulder as Riven comes back down, "All settled in?" she asks curiously.

Riven grins as she walks over and jumps down on the bench beside Dawn taking Dawn's wine from her hand and sipping from it herself, "Yep, although, I think I gave her advice about how fortunate we all are. I'm not sure she really understands, and now I am not sure if I should have." Riven says taking another rather large gulp of Dawn's wine.

Dawn smiles comfortingly, "As my mother once said, being a mother is a learning experience, it will take us both time to get used to having her around, and what to show and teach her when and where." Dawn says as she leant over giving Riven a little kiss on the cheek before taking her wine back and finishing it off for herself. "But that is a good lesson, she is a woman adopted into, well, we aren't quite a nobility, but you are a Consul, and well I am engaged to a Lord of the Empire. My sister, your cousin is the Countess of Corillium and she is surrounded by very powerful women. And sadly, we are few and far between. She needs to understand that this is not the norm. Yet." Dawn says letting out a little sigh as she rests her head on Riven's shoulder.

"Society isn't as fair to us as we would like, but then, all we can do is prepare her for that and make sure she knows what to fight for, and what to strive for when the time comes." Dawn paused then add, "Well, that and guide her towards our own way of thinking just a bit." Dawn teases.

Riven laughs and shakes her head, "That we will, although not too soon. She is far too innocent and adorable for us to corrupt her just yet." she responds in kind and shakes her head again, resting it on Dawn's in turn, reaching for the wine bottle and topping up their shared glass. "What do you suppose will happen with, well, all of this, when you wed your fiance? You will effectively become his." Riven points out looking at Dawn with some concern.

Rolling her eyes, "You know me better than that Riven, I am my own person, besides he loves me, and I have him well and truly wrapped around my, well, sometimes I believe it's me wrapped around him but..." Dawn trails off and just grins teasingly, "Well, perhaps that story can be told another time." she teases.

Riven nudges Dawn, "I am serious Dawn, we adopted Ameliana together, and we bought and built this house together, things are changing with your fiance moving in with us. Where does it leave all of us?" she asks curiously, taking a sip of the wine.

Dawn nods her head, "Well, Regulus will become a father figure to Ameliana, while I have great faith in the pair of us, to raise her. She needs that in her life. I know I am thankful to have had a father in my life, even though I knew that he wasn't mine. I still love him." she says with a fond smile, "We will wed and all live here. This house is huge and has plenty of room for us all, and I will do my duty to my husband, and sire him an heir. More importantly, Ameliana will have a sibling to play with." Dawn says smiling fondly, "And of course, you will always be here with me, and with her." she says giving Riven's cheek a reassuring kiss before taking a sip of the wine herself.

Riven raises her eyebrow slightly skeptically, "Well, while I do love the picture you painted, the fact remains, you are marrying into another family Dawn, one that hails from the Saar highlands, and we both know the Septimus' stance on slavery." Riven paused then add, "Also, you are marrying a man. He is never going to be faithful to you, he already isn't."

Dawn laughs softly, "True that we do, but we are also fortunate to live in a city that has outlawed slavery. In the future, I am sure all the lands of Corillium will follow suit. Although the Empire as a whole does not share the Count's and Countess' outlook on the practice, it's a part of our society, as is my husband taking mistresses." she says a little begrudgingly, "Well." she shrugs slightly, "if I asked him, he would stop. It's just I won't because I love him and I know having a release gives him joy." she says softly nursing the cup a little before a teasing smile crosses her lips, "What I really want is that there wasn't the double standard, sure a lord can take a mistress, but if a lady even looks at another man the wrong way heavens help the lady." Dawn tsks softly shaking her head laughing a little and adds, "Although that doesn't stop me flirting, it's fun to see him get protective and possessive over me." she smiles again, "That and the attention I get is nice, it's a part of who I am I suppose." she shrugs slightly.

Riven just rolls her eyes, "You are just mad, I didn't let you keep that cute legionnaire we met."

Dawn gasps in mock offence, "Me? Be attracted to another man? Unheard of." she scoffs before bursting into laughter, "Okay, I admit it. He was cute, but besides I have all I want in this house." she exclaims waving her hand around the room. "Well, here and currently outside the house," she added as an afterthought.

Riven raises her eyebrow a little and shakes her head, "You are insatiable Dawn." she teases shaking her head.

Dawn nods her head, "And why shouldn't I be? I worked hard to get where I am, and so did you. Why should we not be able to have the same privileges as the men do?" she pauses then pouts a little, "That's right we are women." she whines softly.

Riven just rolls her eyes, at Dawn's philosophical spiel as she takes a sip of the wine and wraps one arm around Dawn, "So, that business you brought up?" she says with a small smirk.

Dawn looks back at Riven, "Oh that! You'll just have to find out." she teases.

Riven rolls her eyes before pushing Dawn down and tackling her, "Nope. I want to know now!" she demands in a playful fashion.

Dawn yelps as she is tackled, before laughing softly as she is held down, "Fine, fine I will tell you." she teases before leaning up slightly to whisper into Riven's ear.

Riven's eyes light up at what she hears and she simply grins at Dawn.